This stinky book belongs to:

_____

_____

_____

For Jimmy James and Rosie ~ SL

For Tom and Sam ~ BC

LITTLE TIGER PRESS
An imprint of Magi Publications
1 The Coda Centre, 189 Munster Road,
London SW6 6AW
www.littletigerpress.com

First published in Great Britain 2003
as **3, 2, 1 Bedtime**
This edition published 2009

A CIP catalogue record for this book is
available from the British Library

Printed in Belgium

10 9 8 7 6 5 4 3 2

SUPER SPUD
AND THE Stinky
Space Rescue!

Sam Lloyd　　Ben Cort

LITTLE TIGER PRESS
London

In a galaxy far, far away,
Spud's alien friends were
getting ready for bed.
"Rip roaring rockets!" Spud
gasped. "What a mess!
They need my help!"
This was a mission for . . .

POW! SLAM! Spud landed on planet Whiff.

"Rip roaring rockets!" he gasped. "What a stink!"

"Pong, pong, pong," nodded the aliens. "We need a bath. Will you help us?"

So Spud washed and scrubbed and
scrubbed and washed until the aliens
were all clean and ready for bed.

"Nighty, nighty, sleepy tighty," whispered Spud. But his mission was not complete. Spud fired up his rocket.

3, 2, 1, BLAST OFF!

SUPERHERO SPACEBOY SPUD TO THE RESCUE!

POW! SLAM! Spud landed on planet Fuzz.

"Rip roaring rockets!" he gasped. "What a tangle!"

"Frizz, frizz, frizz," squeaked the alien. "Will you help me brush my hair?"

So Spud brushed and combed and
combed and brushed until the alien's
hair was neat and tidy, ready for bed.

"Nighty, nighty, sleepy tighty," whispered Spud. But his mission was not complete. Spud fired up his rocket.

3, 2, 1, BLAST OFF!

SUPERHERO SPACEBOY SPUD TO THE RESCUE!

POW! SLAM! Spud landed

on planet Piddle.

"Rip roaring rockets!" he gasped.

"What an awful accident!"

"Pee, pee, pee," nodded the

aliens. "We need to do a wee.

Help us, Super Spud!"

So Spud helped the little
aliens to go to the toilet.

"Nighty, nighty, sleepy tighty," whispered Spud. But still his mission was not complete. Spud fired up his rocket.

3, 2, 1, BLAST OFF!

SUPERHERO SPACEBOY SPUD TO THE RESCUE!

POW! SLAM! Spud landed
on planet Fang.

"Rip roaring rockets!" he gasped.
"Those teeth are filthy! You need
to clean them."

"Gnash, gnash, gnash," nodded
the alien with a smile.

So Spud brushed and polished
and polished and brushed until
the alien's teeth were shiny
and sparkling, ready for bed.

At last the mission was complete. All the aliens were tucked up in bed.

"Nighty, nighty, sleepy . . . tighty . . ."

yawned Spud and climbed on his rocket.

Spud curled up snug in his own bed.
"Well done," smiled his mummy.
"It's a tough job being a superhero."
She leaned forward and gave
him a kiss. "Nighty, nighty, sleepy
tighty," she whispered . . .

But Superhero Spaceboy Spud
was already fast asleep.

The end

More stinky books
from Little Tiger Press!

For information regarding any of the above titles or
for our catalogue, please contact us: Little Tiger Press,
1 The Coda Centre, 189 Munster Road, London SW6 6AW
Tel: 020 7385 6333, Fax: 020 7385 7333, E-mail: info@littletiger.co.uk
www.littletigerpress.com